LOVE BETWEEN 2 BOOBS

Irene D. Thomas

Table Of Contents

Chapter 1

Sometimes you simply want to get fucked by someone you've never met before.

You shower when it's already dark. You put on your clothes. You go, your fists stuffed into your jacket pockets. You move rapidly, pressing your heels into the pavement, and you keep your head down. You already know where you're heading.

There's a club nearby. You must be aware of its location. You go down the lane until you reach the second door on the left, which leads to the basement.

Cabs are pulling up and letting passengers out and letting other people stumble in. The river can be smelled from here, and it does not smell pleasant.

Take out the pack of smokes and strike it on your hand before returning it to your pocket unopened. and proceed.

Down the stairs and to the bar; you order a neat scotch and drink it quickly. The term "electronic commerce" refers to the sale of electronic goods. She is not present. She would never be here. And that's why you are here now.

Who is it going to be? Find someone who seems like she can take you, and gaze, head tilted down. Look up at her with your brow furrowed and your eyes wide and begging. The first one will look away. It's fine. Let her look aside, and locate another one.

The correct one will gaze back. The proper person will understand what this implies. The right one will look you in the eyes and then head to the bar to get a drink. And you'll order another drink, but this time you'll sip it. Squeeze the glass tightly in your palm, as if attempting to shatter it, then drink slowly. Allow the alcohol to rest on your tongue and burn a bit before swallowing it. Allow her to observe you.

Look for her again once you finish your drink. Turn around and leave a tip on the bar. You must push your way past the mob. You will feel her grip your elbow before you make it to the door. Allow her to stop you.

She drags you back toward the bar but continues going. There are further steps to the left that go to a deeper basement. Stone butches are playing pool, and if you come too close to one, you'll get the crap knocked out of you, and not in the manner you want.

She's going to fetch her coat. She throws you up against the cinder-block wall and grinds her knee between your legs as you turn around. It's difficult to breathe as she presses into you, forcing you between her and the wall. She's sucking your tongue. I'm sucking your tongue instead of kissing you; everything is whirling.

"Let's go," she says, and you do.

She walks straight by the cabs outside. The roadway is pitch black. People are fucking in the doorways, but she continues going. At the river's edge, there is a chain-link fence. As you're flung against it, the sound of it shocks you, the metal rippling like a wave along the deserted streets in thunderous smashes.

She yanks up your shirt, her lips briefly on your breasts before turning you around and pushing you against the hard metal. She grabs your belt and yanks your pants down to your knees. As she fumbles with you, the links in the fence pinch on your tummy and your breasts. You lift your hands up and wrap your fingers firmly, clutching to the barrier and letting her yank on you.

She bites your neck; you can feel her injuring you. She wets her fingers on your cunt. Between your legs, move one hand, then both hands. She pushes a moist finger into your ass, grinding her hips into you and sliding her hand and body into you. Her other hand, her full hand, is on your cunt. She's scrubbing you. You want her to fill you, but you don't have a choice right now.

You hear a vehicle and suddenly you're in the headlights for a split second as a taxi pulls a U-turn and drives away. She's giggling. "Thcy won't even know what they were looking at: people fucking, maybe, but

females or boys? They'll presume they're guys.
The notion of being caught in the spotlight drives you insane. You want to leave. You want her to get you off, but you don't want this to end.
She bends her knees and wraps herself around you. Still fucking you in the ass, she eventually presses her other hand into your cunt, and you instantly feel yourself opening up for her. More fingers go inside you and yet you want more. You want her within you all the way to her wrist. You want her whole fist into you.
You're now perched on the precipice, your body giving way and the muscles in your arms straining and keeping you up. The cold metal fence cuts into your fingertips as your arms start to quiver. "You're shouting," she remarks, amused. a misplace. Tonight you became absolutely disoriented. That's exactly what you needed.
No numbers or names are exchanged. "I don't want to get fucked," she continues,

"but that was entertaining." She then walks away.

Chapter 2

They came from miles to be here, I thought as I feel the car's tires scrunch on the gravel road. Peering through the rain-washed windshield I recall what you told me. You sat in my kitchen, a beam of sunshine on your hair and lips, an island of joy in this quiet, open, and empty space. You grinned at me, knowing that every dirty word you spoke was twisting my heart as you informed me when and where to turn up. I wasn't sure whether you were joking or not. Now I'm here, nervous at the prospect of discovering the truth, and I want to call you in your new home with him and tell you that I've gone, after all, to see whether it hurts you.

The establishment is your typical English rural pub, too far out of town for a former city person like myself to walk there. The Horse and Hounds are square, brick and thatch, with a cracked wooden sign hanging and creaking above the entrance. It might

have been any bar in the nation, but you—my darling, taunting, unattainable you—told me it was unique.
"They're coming from all over the county for a little, you know..." you added, peering at me from the corner of your cat's eyes. I am aware. I had seen that expression on your face before when your head lay on my pillow. It was a look that conveyed happiness; private, unique pleasure. You told me about what occurred that night at the bar while holding a coffee cup in my bed, one eye on the clock since you knew your spouse would be home for dinner in an hour, and that it would happen again. You were gone a week or two later, and I immediately realized why you had instructed me to go there: to soothe the agony of your departure.

When I come in, putting a newspaper over my head to catch the rain, I am struck by two things: the scorching, dog-like scent of pubs now that smoking is prohibited, and the women's inconspicuousness. I chastised myself for my foolishness. Had I imagined them seated behind a banner? That would have made you laugh, in that high, sighing, skipping chuckle that made your throat work magnificently.

I make my way to the bar, fluttering my wet paper and yanking my coat open. I order a bitter shandy from the barmaid, a squat, middle-aged lady dripping in bangles and earrings, and take a minute to study the ladies.

A group of six ladies sits at a table in the furthest corner, half concealed in a nook in the wall. As I taste the first glug of warm, earthy beer, I notice the age difference between them all. There is a lady going straight for sixty if she is a day, but another who can't be older than twenty-two. I inwardly smack myself for making assumptions once again. Did I expect them to all resemble me?

The term "electronic commerce" refers to the sale of electronic goods. I can see, as I go past the fireplace on the red, sticky carpet, the mark of loneliness on their faces. It's the type of loneliness that clings to a woman's features like moss or cobwebs; the kind of loneliness that accumulates over time in this dreary location that the rain never leaves alone. It's the kind of loneliness that a chat at the post office, a husband's hand, or the glow of the TV can't take away; the loneliness of a woman surrounded by love but unable to love, and who feels her heart is beating loudly and alone in all these wide open spaces; not thrumming in time with the world or someone else. My face looks like theirs now, after you left my heartbeat to slow alone.

When I arrive at the table, the lady in charge, Justine, looks up and grins. We had a strained chat on the phone a day or two ago to clarify the timings. She is approximately forty, with black hair, and a stylish wax jacket on her small body. I can tell by her accent and the somewhat arrogant way she looks at her small group that she is a former urbanite like myself, and affluent to boot.

We exchange hellos. I hadn't really considered what to say next, but happily, someone is pushing a chair over and another is walking along to make room, and there I am, sat among them with the least amount of trouble. They don't want to bring attention to themselves. I feel as though I've just started a new book club.

The discussion also had the vibe of a book club. It's the jittery, impolite chatter of ladies who want to make a good impression. I take it all in. Justine used to be something glamorous in the city until she and her husband upped sticks to the country to have a kid. It is apparent from the way she is accustomed to exercising authority. Kim, the younger one, is fat and mousey, and she has a kid at home with her farmworker husband. She's a local who has just recently left the county. Marge is a weathered lady in her late fifties whose boyfriend, who died last year, is often mentioned in non-gender-specific ways. There are two thirtysomething pals, Sam and Lisa, with matching shiny hair- cuts and stylish Ugg boots. To me, it is painfully evident that they are lovers and believe it is a secret. Then there is a wiry, clear-skinned lady of undetermined age, dressed boyishly in jeans and a checkered shirt, her blonde hair trimmed tight to her head and her hands writhing for want of a cigarette.

This is where I insert my tale. The term "electronic commerce" refers to the sale of electronic goods. No, nobody was back at the cottage I purchased petulantly, figuring I was too old to need city distractions anymore. What should I do? Well, I'm a writer. The term "responsibility" refers to the act of determining whether or not a person is responsible for his or her own actions. I left out how I had despised the apartment straightaway but remained because after living next door for six weeks, you arrived in my kitchen and then in my bed, and then came over every day at 12:00

to drink coffee and make love while your husband worked without thinking about you. I forgot to note that after he got the new job, you refused to make any arrangements to meet me again as if making plans gave our affair some type of calculation while sliding through my back door every day you appeared to be able to pass off as a series of one-off mistakes of judgment. Then you vanished, leaving flowers on the kitchen table while the moving truck belched and shuddered away.

He was attempting to get you pregnant, but you didn't want him to. You claimed the sensation of my skin on yours made you feel like a woman and not a reproductive machine consisting of fluids and membranes. Then you abandoned me in this rural hell, and I'm still hurting.

I watch for a time, keeping everything to myself. The conversation leans toward neutral themes like the weather, the TV, and the final nice fair of the summer. It is not arousing yet my intestines are buzzing with frantic excitement. You'd told me about this tiny group, and now that I can't have you, I want to live in the narrative you'd left behind.

You can't recall how it occurred the previous time, you whispered, lying on one elbow in bed, your hair soft and straggly from my hands. You said, sliding a finger from my chin to my breastbone, it truly was a book club to start with. The term "independent" refers to a person who does not work for the government. Perhaps it was because they were all lonely at the same moment, or because the appropriate quantity of chardonnay was consumed. You said that many causes contributed to an incident. The term "electronic commerce" refers to the sale of electronic goods. They didn't say much about it after that, you grinned as you kissed me, but months later Justine sent out an email saying the "book club" was meeting again. "You should try it," you urged, seeming unhappy for reasons I didn't understand at the time.

I had arrived there about half an hour before the final orders, trying to limit any uncomfortable chitchat. The bell rings at 11:00 p.m., and Maureen, the barmaid, begins throwing the locals out with a ringing singsong of "Finish up, guys!" As she trundles by with a towel and a bottle of anti-bac spray, Maureen slips a key surreptitiously onto the table in front of Justine. Nobody else in the bar would have seen her do it, but we hear the soft click of the key on the wood and the atmosphere goes up a notch. I see them becoming increasingly tense. Justine, who is accustomed to being watched, downs the vodka and orange she has been nursing, and everyone else follows suit. Jen, the boyish blonde, prepares by tucking a roll-up cigarette behind her ear. Maureen nods to us as the final punter goes and she locks the doors behind him. Justine zips up her wax coat and grins at us, but her smile is different this time. It's not the wide-mouthed, happy smile of earlier, but a slight, sneaky, knowing twist of the lips.

Without saying a word, we got up and went with her to the side entrance, where we exit into the space between the bar and its outside walls. I borrow a light from Jen as the others pass by. I ask, "What's in it for Maureen?" as we both exhale.

Jen steps up and adds quietly, "Last time she joined us." "But not tonight."

Jen's tone indicates that the time for chitchat has gone and that all of my queries will be addressed in other ways, despite the fact that I want to start a dialogue. I follow her into the shadows while smoking heavily in the chilly night air.

The six of us sneak into the woods behind the tavern via the dense grass at the rear. I have to keep an eye on Jen's coat to remain on the path between the trees as the lights from the bar kitchen start to dim. My palms and the back of my neck are chilled by the chilly air and rain-drenched leaves. As I feel the dirt sticky beneath my feet in the darkness, I start to feel uneasy. I believe that this is how victims wind up dismembered in someone's vehicle trunk. Jen then takes a quick look behind her to make sure I'm still there. Her chin's powerful curvature and the way her neck's nape hair is trimmed both appeals to me. I follow when I have a hazy, fundamental desire flutter.

We continue walking until we arrive at a large shed with brick walls covered in brown paint that is flaking. Justine unlocks the door and steps inside after casting a cunning to peek up the muddy walk. I can smell the inside from where I'm standing at the rear of the crowd: soil, dried leaves, paint, and wood. We entered them in alphabetical order.

Until Justine turns on a camping gas lamp and a few candles that are resting on an old, cracked coffee table, the inside is gloomy. Around the compact, low areas are several moist pillows and moth-eaten carpets. Cross-legged on the ground, we sit.

All of us feel the pressure of the environment. There is a pervasive sensation of yearning in the space as if our shared desires are overflowing onto one another. Expectation, a tinge of desire, and something like cannibalism predominate. I'm aware that everyone is watching me. Kim and Marge are graciously glancing down at me, while Sam and Lisa are resisting the impulse to prod each other and point in my direction. Jen is giving me a strong, butch evaluation that normally I would find offensive, but in this situation, it would be rude to protest.

Justine gives me a neutral grin and puts her hand on my arm. She seems to be the one who is most at ease with what is going to occur.

She responds, "I know a buddy told you to come along." Did she explain what occurred the previous time? She gives my shoulder a slow, steady squeeze.

You did inform me. You stated, "I ended up taking everything off and sitting in the center of them." You exhaled, your hand following your thoughts and mine following yours, "I showed them how I do it when I'm alone."

Justine nods encouragingly as I start to take the buttons off my coat. After that, I hesitate, unsure of how and whether to continue. I now understand that whatever female Jen is obsessing about must have been adored as she kneels closer to me and takes off my shoes with such tenderness and assurance. Jen had been reclining back in the shadows.

My shirt and jeans are removed. While doing so, I find it difficult to look anybody in the eye, despite the fact that I can see Marge's arm curved almost protectively over Kim's shoulders and Sam and Lisa holding hands. I see you undressing in front of these ladies here in the chilly weather, and I get a rush from echoing you since it seems to draw you nearer to me.

I can feel the pent-up desire my still-young body naturally produces, as well as the ingrained dread of other women looking at my body and—most of all—the crushing sense of futility that has pervaded everything since you vanished. I've stopped.

Marge is the one who jolts me out of it this time. She waits for me to glance up before catching my sight. She has blue eyes and a steely gray complexion, a reliably beautiful face. She has a pleasant West Country burr and a rich speaking voice.

Chickadee, it's only flesh and blood, she cries. You don't need to provide us with anything else.

She simultaneously sounds kind and desirous. I want to expose my body to her—this weeping, elderly woman—in order to compare her suffering to mine. Grief is so near to becoming a passion that the idea of sharing it makes me squirm out of my underpants before I can alter my mind.

In a pitch-black room with six other ladies, I'm nude. This is your fault, I say. You constantly force me to do actions that I wouldn't normally do. I've been living every

second of the last year as if you were watching me, even during the times when we weren't together, and it has made me happier. The hundreds of love letters I've written to you, whether or not they were delivered, are the greatest work I've ever produced. I haven't written a word of the book I set out to write. Without your drawing me more clearly, like an artist polishing her work, I would not have been able to do it.
Jen is giving me the drought-stricken lady staring at a lake expression. She is chivalrous, quiet, powerful, and trim. Her shoulders are slender and muscular, and I can see the scowl that quiet, gloomy ladies often sport. I didn't know how to desire a woman until you showed me how. Wanting her is simple, so I do. I choose to entertain her.
I put my hand on my neck, tracing my fingers down to my collarbone, and moan as my palm's recognizable lines brush across my breast. If this is too hasty or coy for the

company, I wonder. I turn to face Justine, who has taken off her coat and undone the button of her denim. She is still smiling at us all while reclining on a pillow, and her hand is idly traced around her navel.

I now bring my hands to my hips. You liked holding my hips.

You often entered my kitchen the day we had our first sexual encounter, and as I stood there brewing coffee with my back to you, you remarked that I had model-like proportions. Unsure whether it was an unintentional insult or genuine praise, I laughed loudly. My world came crashing down when your hands were on my hips and your breath was on my neck.

I briefly get lost in myself as my hips nestle gently into my hands as horse chestnuts nestle into their silken casings. I hear a sigh—I'm not sure whose it is—and am aware of the ladies once again as my hand moves up my thigh and then to the softest flesh where my legs converge.

They appear in flashes as I gaze up. The tiny hand of Justine, who is ahead of me, is moving fluidly into her pants. Sam and Lisa are gingerly kissing, as if it is the first time, and nibbling nervously at each other's lips. Marge is now holding Kim in a tight bear embrace after Kim shifts to allow Marge to cradle her over her lap. Jen is still and silently observing me with her head tilted to the side and her arms around her knees. I set out on a quest to get her. I tilt my head back and spread my fingers over my cunt in an effort to get her to respond.

I can see you right here. You observe me, as you have done a hundred times in bed, as the thick bulb of my middle finger presses into my clit, then moves to a thin, vivid seam, then to the deep aperture below, before easing and tasting. I am conscious of the smile that is rolling over my mouth—the one you first saw when you pointed it out to me. In the back of her throat, Jen chuckles. She had previously seen that smirk on the face of a person she loves. When I open my eyes, she is crawling toward me on the uneven floor as I become comfortable with the easy beat of my fingers.

As she approaches me, I see that everyone else in the area is starting to relax, almost as if they are in a trance. The most vulnerable are Sam and Lisa, whose love is so obvious and so close to the surface. Sam has taken Lisa's scarf and top off of her and is giving her thousands of adoring kisses on the neck and shoulders. They are only here because they need this hidden insanity to completely reveal themselves to one another, and they only have eyes for one another.

Marge is holding Kim's heated round face with her lovely, leathery brown hands—hands that have hugged the same lady for years. Kim is gazing up at Marge with a kind of unbelievably joyful delight. Kim pulls up her own skirt and gives her own wide, curving legs the attention her husband struggles to provide. Justine has taken off her shirt and pants and is lavishly and freely stroking herself.

On all fours, Jen approaches me with grace and curiosity. I wonder whether she wants me to turn to her and stop harming myself. Though I am unaware of the parts we are all playing, I can tell by the way she is curled up next to me that she is seldom, if ever, "done." She obviously enjoys making other people feel good because of the way her eyes dart from my hand to my curled toes to the blush that starts to rise up my neck. She is awaiting approval.

She extends her hand as I nod. She runs a frigid fingertip across my starving lips. My lips tremble at her touch since I haven't been kissed in what seems like a very long time. She crouched down to the arc of my breast and starts moving her lips and tongue slowly and expertly over my flesh. I exhale, focusing just on the feeling before thinking about her, then you. As she moves to lay next to me, her lips enclose my nipple and her tongue makes slow circles around it, sucking more forcefully. I pull her closer to me as I reach out reflexively to rub the silky hair on the back of her neck. Justine responds to her gentle moan with a little half-laugh. She is the one Jen is lusting over, I know as I watch her closely observe Jen.

As I observe them, I notice that the atmosphere in the room is becoming heavier and more intense. Sam and Lisa are trapped against each other on the floor, their arms and legs intertwined. They are passionately kissing while their hips are grinding against each other. Kim's quiet panting can be heard as Marge continues to cradle the younger lady while also inserting her hand within. Kim is fixated as she observes Jen and me. I close my eyes and listen to them all, the rhythmic sounds of hands on flesh and lips on lips, nearly attempting to identify the unique noises you created only for me.

Jen ascends above me. Her gentle but persistent mouth is on mine. She smells like damp grass and cheap soap, and I can taste alcohol and cigarettes in her. I feel like betraying us, but then I see you with him and I put my legs around Jen's waist.

She is breathing heavily on my neck as her belt feels chilly against my thighs. I reach below her shirt and yank at the buttons. Knowing that she won't like being touched, I firmly press her breast. She gives herself permission to hunch her back and moan. She differs from you. She feels heavy, rough, and grumpy. In my arms, you were like sunshine. I want her to penetrate me, to surround me with grotesque feelings, and to eject you. I shove myself hard and moist against her trousers while encircling her neck with both of my arms. I snarl, "Fuck me," into her ear as she pushes back.

The words heighten the tense atmosphere in the room. Kim had lifted her knees and opened her legs wide as Marge crushes her whole palm firmly on her cunt. Lisa kneels between Sam's legs, kissing and grasping her hips while Sam lies on her back, hands over her lips. Justine is on her knees, her hand working quickly and her gaze fixed on us.

Jen's fingers press into me, and I lose track of time for a few seconds. She pauses inside me, allowing me to stiffen around her hand before beginning to push back and forth. She drives her palm harder with the force in her hips and back, her whole body moving in a seamless wave. She has her eyes closed and lips wide in an attitude of utter indifference. I'm curious whether she's envisioning someone else underneath her, and that drives me on. I imagine you fucking me like this and my body reacts with another wave of pleasure but my heart cringes. The term "electronic commerce" refers to the sale of electronic goods. I wrap my legs around her and press my clit against her belt buckle. I'm fiercely pushing against her, forcing her to fuck me harder with her hand locked between us, and she loves it.

In a nook there I hear someone coming. I can't identify who it is since my eyes are closed, but I can hear the rushing surge of hips and hands reaching a climax, then slowing and intensifying, then fading away. It acts on the rest of us like magic. Kim gives out a series of shocked, ecstatic gasps as Justine starts to make a low, humming sound in the back of her throat. The forbidden sound of another woman's most secret pleasure combines with my own, and I start to feel the familiar strain in my legs and stomach.

As I build to my orgasm, sensible, reasoned ideas are pushed away and bizarre visions burst loose in my head. In my thoughts, I picture hands, tongues, breasts, and shoulder blades moving to my beat. I see myself in snatches. I'm curious whether any of these ladies fucked you like this, and the concept sticks with you. In my mind's eye the ladies are in this room exactly as they are in reality but below Jen, bucking and gasping is you, not me. In my imagination, I see you with a drop of perspiration clinging to your hair that falls over your eyes, your head thrown back, your toes crossed in that manner you do when you're lost in it all. My brain filled with echoes of your screams and I think I can smell you. My body tightens and I yell, half delight, half misery, and shiver into completion. Jen places her hand over my lips to keep me silent, and I scream pleasure and anguish into her palm.

I can't recall what happened right after, but we're all clothed, a bit tired, and splitting up in the parking lot. Justine is the only one that catches everyone's attention. Jen gives her a thoughtful look but says nothing to anybody. I nod and walk away.

Driving home, too fatigued to weep, I wonder whether I will go back again. I'm not sure whether this is helping or harming me. You thought it would cure me and teach me now that you're gone, but I'm not sure I'll ever be able to make love to someone without you in my brain.

I'm so exhausted when I get in my driveway that I nearly forget to lock the vehicle. I come to a halt as I drag myself to the front door. You're shivering and red-eyed, sitting gravely on the threshold beneath the porch light. My head fizzes when you stare at me. I make a move to speak, but you respond with your eyes, imploring, dark, and regretful.

"Is it too late?" you ask as I stumble to the front door. I collapse to my knees alongside you on the step, unable to speak, and shake my head.

Chapter 3

So I'm a sucker for old butches. Sue me.

Okay, not that old. Older. Somewhere about sixty. A true butch. You know the kind I'm referring to. They're a dying breed.

The youngest ones are nearly fifty, and the oldest...well, they'll stay hard butch as long as they live. Not made of stone. No, I don't mean the actual transmen who didn't have all the current choices for transition. I'm talking about the actual butches. Men's clothes and chivalry. Short, spiky hair that is commonly flecked with gray. As often as not, they're wearing women's underwear, whatever sort their moms forced them to wear.

And that's how they are: tough and macho on the surface, delicate and feminine on the inside. They have names like Laurie, Julianne, and Caroline, and they're either too old to bother changing their names to tough names like AJ, Sam, and Drake, or they're somewhere in the middle where they took on hippy names like Bear, Blue Jay, and Sunny.

Everything about elder butches appeals to me. I like how they'll open a door for me and then gaze at my a$$ when I go through. But yet, when I attempt to catch them at it, they're staring me in the eye every time. I adore how they'll get up to do anything physical for me, even though I'm younger and could do it just as well. I like how they each have their own area of skill that demonstrates they're a successful part of a man's world, whether it's motorbikes, line cookery, accountancy, or anything with animals. I adore how they'll squish a spider one minute and then scream like a young girl the next over a snake. I like the way they walk, with a male conviction and swagger and a feminine delicate stride. And I like how they feel: powerful arms and hands with a hint of softness in the center. I adore how they can do all the things a guy can do, all while making me feel like the center of their world. And I appreciate how, when things go tough, they're strong enough to depend on someone instead of pretending they can do it all on their own.

You understand my point, don't you? I adore a true butch. And I love to make love to a true butch.

Every year, I attend this women's meeting. The answer is yes. It's a small writer's retreat where we all get to know one other gradually over time. A few new women arrive each time, but there are many of us who have been attending for years and will continue to do so if we can.

I go to this retreat every six months to fawn over the butches. Laurie, who looks so much like a guy that you have to do a second take when she opens her lips and has the voice of a little woman, is one of them. Bear can make a dish and serve it with a grin; she's petite and dressed like a 1950s greaser. Sunny, whose eyes melt me, arrives with her high femme boyfriend, and they sell ice from an ancient ice cream truck.

I like pretending to write on the rock wall outside the dining hall while watching people go about their business. I like flirting with them from across the salad bar. I love to accidentally bump into them. Feel their hands on my shoulders and gaze into their eyes as they apologize despite the fact that they are not to blame. I like to make fun of them for not going swimming on the warmest days when all the ladies and soft butches are already in the water.

I've been enjoying these retreats for a lot of years but this year things have changed. There are no cliques at this retreat. Lunchtime arrives, and we all sit together haphazardly. Laurie takes the seat directly across from me this time. It's the first time I've really communicated with her. We chat about what we write, where we live, and what we do for a living. I inquire about her thoughts on a composition I may read at the evening open mic session. She enjoys it. We both move to change the page at the same moment, and her hand touches mine.

I'm already ablaze. I haven't been with a lady in far too long. I see a flush on her cheeks and wonder whether it's reciprocal. I offer to share a few additional things; it's an opening of myself with no danger to her. She bites, so we pick a quiet place with some uncomfortable seats (because there are no comfortable chairs at the retreat).

I see her reading as her eyes skim the words and her expression shifts gradually in response to the poetry. I'm simply enjoying this little portion of Laurie that is all mine because I'm not foolish enough to aspire for more.

When she's done, she beams. for some time sits. We discuss the works, when I wrote them, for whom, and if they still reflect reality. She claims she wants to know more about me. Can she take me to supper with her? I resist the impulse to shout "Hooray!"

and instead respond with a subdued, as-feminine-as-I-can-get "Yes."
She invites me to a meal. Good chat, a relaxed setting, and plenty of eye contact. She makes a remark about the way I hold my knife and fork in a European manner, never putting the knife down. Taking my hand, she. I can sense her heartbeat. Or maybe it's my own voice, which is pounding in my throat.
She embraces me when we are back at the retreat. She has her whole body pressed up against me, which at first seems too chaste. I encircle her and can feel the muscles in her back tensing as she moves. Her breasts are pressing on me.
I'm not a fool; I know how I should play: let the genuine butches make the decisions. I want more. Women provide their services. They wriggle their asses, thrust out their breasts, and bat their eyelids while unintentionally brushing their hands along exposed flesh. They wink if they're very bold. They do all these actions to express

their interest in the butch, but the butch must initiate contact. If anybody is to blame, it is the butch since she must assume the danger.

I'm not the typical femme. I follow my own set of rules, giving the butch just enough authority to feel secure and taking just enough power to feel in charge. I strive to completely disappear into the gaps between us as I press my whole body up against hers. As we separate, I grasp her hand. I turn around and give her a sincere, in-your-face thank you for a fantastic, if rather brief, evening. I grin. I never wink.

The next night, I do my open-mike segment in front of Laurie. After, volunteers provide a late-night snack, and as she passes me to get to the end of the line, she brushes into me. She then sits down with a few of her pals as I do the same. But across the room, our eyes continue to lock. I don't glance down till after she does. I'm not running; she is undoubtedly chasing.

Late hour. I give my buddies hugs and go out into the cold evening air. The retreat contains a dining hall and many tiny, basic hotel-style cabins. Large starlit spaces between the cottages and minimal porch lights provide for a nice nighttime stroll amongst the structures. Tonight begins like way, and then all of a sudden I'm warm. Actually hot.

I get a call from Laurie. I turn to see her stroll over to me. Although I want to reach out and touch her, I refrain. She follows me as I turn to go toward my cabin.

Can I take you to your accommodation on foot? Her female voice is powerful. She's not really asking me a question so much as giving me a chance to intervene before things go out of hand.

I would enjoy that. I want things to take a wrong turn.

We enter my room, and I wait outside for her to enter. To eliminate the possibility of interruption, I lock the door. Maybe she's attempting to comprehend a femme my age,

which may be pushing things a little too far. She is approximately 20 years older than I am.
She beams. I had planned to do that.
At the moment, I'm shy. I don't often blush, but I'm doing it now. But I don't need to be afraid. She is a true butch and has situational awareness.
Could I hold you? She greets me with outstretched arms while still standing.
I cross the room three steps to her, and she enfolds me in her arms. Her lips touch mine as my head is cocked upward. She is just slightly taller than I am, just enough for me to notice our physical differences. I'm reminded of the parallels by her kiss. She has the gentle fullness of a genuine lady on her lips. She has big feet and is supporting me with her powerful arms, which is a good thing since I may otherwise trip and fall.
The kiss is passionate. The tongues and lips are hot and moist. My hand is on her face, and as we kiss, I can feel her jaw moving. Nothing else exists. Only this kiss remains.

She takes a little step back and exhales, "Wow!" before diving right back in for more. We have long kisses. No, I am aware that is untrue. We kiss for what seems like hours, just sensing the other's response. I feel her reach for the hem of my shirt and raise it after what seems like a lifetime. I make a motion to make things simpler, letting the shirt fall over my head while I watch her release it gradually so that it will land on the ground. My nipples pucker when the chilly air from the open window brushes my skin. In the faint glow from the porch light, I wasn't sure she could see that, but as she puts out a hand to touch one of them, I shudder.

Then I became bashful once again. For sex, I like to be clean. I also appreciate it when my partner is tidy. I ask, putting on my most subdued feminine expression, "Shower?"

With a nod. he grabs my hand and leads me into the restroom. Short showers are provided. We don't even attempt to share it since there is only one stall. When I'm sufficiently dry and primed to suit my standards of a femme, she exits her shower. Through the steam, even in the nearly nonexistent light, I can make out her black nipple pointing at me. It's much too alluring. I crouch down, keeping my eyes on her for as long as I can, and run my tongue over her nipple. She exhales a little before placing her hand behind my head. I keep licking as I hear her moan. I close my lips around her breast and begin sucking. first gently. You can never tell how soft or firm a lady likes it. As her palm grips the back of my neck more firmly, I suck harder. She grunts.

She steps back and releases me.

I allow her space to dry off and use my toiletries whenever she pleases. I'm trying not to move too quickly. Let her dictate the tempo. I back out of the bathroom as she turns to face me once again, stopping not far from where the backs of my knees touch the bed.

She approaches me, and another kiss forms between our bodies. However, there is nothing covering us this time. I'm relieved to have the comfort of the bed after being startled by her flesh touching mine. The intensity of the kiss increases somewhat. Only because no dream feels this lovely do I know that this is not a dream.

Then Laurie begins to seem hesitant. She murmurs, "I don't have anything with me."

Since I am at a loss for words and don't want to overwhelm her, I turn around and reach under the bed to get my toy bag. I usually bring my toys on vacation since you never know when you may need them, even for a solo performance.

After giving the bag a quick glance, she walks by me and places it on the bed. When she takes out the vibrator and dildo, she smiles a little. When she produces my completely adjustable leather harness, she then grinned broadly. Just in case, I brush my breast against her arm as I set the lubrication on the nightstand.

Without wasting any time, Laurie quickly dons the harness and fastens the dildo. She stops and then turns to face me as if I had something to say or do. I go back to my tried-and-true method and take the other nipple in my mouth.

She likes strong suction, and I adore the sensation of her nipple in my mouth. She has very firm breasts. She cleverly flips the script as I reach over to play with the other nipple.

She turns us so that my back is once again towards the bed and then presses down on me to signal that I must be on the bed. Now. I'm already drenched in sweat and my chest is thumping. She gently creeps behind me as I slowly slip back into the bed, all the way up to the pillows.

She may proceed slowly, take her time, and attempt to tease me for hours, I reasoned. But tonight, at least, it's not her style. She opens my legs wide before placing her tongue on my other lips.

Oooooh. first warm, moist tongue contact with my clit.

Nothing else compares to that. She is skilled at what she does. I'll be writhing on the bed in a couple of minutes.

"Please...please..." I humbly request that she move.

And she complies. She penetrates me with the dildo very slowly while kneeling between my legs with her body upright. I could jump into it. However, the way she teases me makes me pant with need and causes my hips to rise up to meet each little longer push.

She fucks me while making varied murmurs and moans. She is skilled at what she does. I want more from her since she is both soft and hard enough. I want more.

She eventually lets herself go as I finally groan that I'm going to come. She lays down on top of me and uses the whole dildo to shove. She gives me another passionate, urgent kiss. Her groan begins to grow as my own orgasm reaches its pinnacle. She gives

out a deep-throated cry to announce her own climax as I descend to the other side.
She begins to try to escape from me, but I keep her in place. She lifts her head just enough to give me a gorgeous grin as I glance in her direction. Her hair is really attractive since it is spiking out in all directions. She softly kisses my lips as well as my cheeks, eyes, and mouth.
Electricity is still available.
It simply takes the slightest movement to trigger her retreat when I'm ready. She walks over and spreads down next to me after taking the harness off and setting it on the bed.

A little while later, I woke up shivering from the open window. I feel warm just seeing Laurie next to me, breathing quietly. I can't help but touch her body with my hand. I let my featherlight fingers flit over her skin's mountains and valleys.

Pale breasts with brown nipples contrast with tanned arms and hands. Although soft, her tummy is flatter than I anticipated.
Her pubic hair is curled tightly and is still moist. As my hand investigates, I can hear her respiration alter, and as I touch those curls, my hand freezes.
I work harder when I get a favorable response. I then tease my curls. I run my fingers down the thigh-to-mons crease. I step away and run my hand along the arc of her hip, then come back and repeat the motions.
She relaxes and lays over on her back, spreading her legs just a little bit. I gently probe again, then slide the tiniest portion of my fingertip along the space between her lips. She grunts. I repeat the process as she watches. Her hands are entirely relaxed, her lips are parted, and her eyes are closed.
She opens up the space between her legs by bending them wider. I have a sneaking suspicion that if I approach her, she would pull away. I tease the flesh by delicately

rubbing it with my fingers. I split her lips a little bit more widely with each repeat until I eventually expose her clit. My moist fingertip barely touched her already-glistening clit after I insert it in my mouth. As she raises her hips into my finger and tucks her head back into the cushions, she utters the most delightful moan. I keep going, each touch as gentle as the last. Every wet crevice is explored by my fingertips. She then raises her hips to enclose them as they approach her aperture.

Desire causes my body to tremble. I wish I could fuck her. She is very vulnerable. So desirous So prepared

She could really want it. Perhaps since she is a true butch, she can't ask for it. won't request it. But maybe, just perhaps, she wants it with the same fervor that I do.

I continue to play with her clit for a minute, removing my fingers to do so, and inserting two of them. She's so drenched.

“Stay. Wait. Believe me. I hurry rapidly away from her, get the dildo and harness, and strap myself in while I beseech her.

She has to hear what I'm doing, but she remains exactly how she is, eyes closed, hands relaxed, hips slowly moving. I was about to mount her, but the sight of her wetness made my lips thirst, and I need to taste her. She's sweet and salty, and she's absolutely dripping. She continues straining her hips higher, looking for something that isn't there yet. So I kneel between her legs and lay the head of the dildo on her clit.

The answer is yes. I want to make certain that she is prepared and willing. She certainly is. She jerks her hips in such a manner that I have no option but to enter her. She wraps her legs around me and makes it apparent, while she never says a word, that she wants to be fucked. Properly. Forcefully. Now.

I never imagined I'd have the honor of fucking a butch. I've had my fancies. This is so much better. She opens her eyes and stares at me once I'm within her. I know she wants it. I know she's all here with me.

I'm fucking her. And she does so gracefully. Her legs were wrapped around my hips, her hands reaching up to pinch one of my nipples, her hips rising to meet every thrust from my hand.

I maintain a tight grip on myself despite the thrusting, groaning, and sweating. I may cum at any time. I only allow myself to come in rhythm with her orgasm when her hands grab the sheets and she exclaims "Yes" once. Something about reaching an orgasm while fucking your boyfriend appeals to me. It's as if a tunnel runs right through the center of me, and the orgasm fills the whole interior area. For a little period, the thrill takes control. It seems like forever, yet it's just a fraction of a second.

When I return to myself, Laurie is letting out the last small sigh from her orgasm.

As soon as she stops swaying, I remove, unhook the strap and let it drop to the floor, and then lay back down on top of her.

I want to shield her from any concerns she may have. But she's all right.
She looks up at me, kisses me, and then pulls me into a fetal position next to her. "I had no idea you could accomplish that. "Did you cum?"
I nod. Was that great... I let the phrase fade away. She nods. "More than fine. You're pretty skilled."
I grin.
We fall asleep till sometime in the early morning when the sky first becomes gray. When I wake up, she is perched on the side of the bed. I sense she wants to return to her room, and I assure her that's OK. We both know this interaction isn't going to lead to something more permanent. Well, save for potentially a repeat performance in six months.
Did I tell you I have a thing for butches?

Chapter 4

She arrived at the classroom late, as usual, a tight black skirt running halfway up her ass. She wore heels practically every day, and today was no exception. If they'd been led, the red heels would have been crisp and pointed enough to be used as pencils. I concentrated on my notepad while watching her black skirt, red shoes, and brown legs, hunching my shoulders behind their light-jacket barrier. In my situation, exposing my flesh was hardly worth the danger.

She was also astute, immediately determining where we were in the conversation and piercing it with words and phrases that were too carefully selected to irritate with their bluntness. This did bother me, of course, and her toes annoyed me as she pulled one shoe off with the other foot, and her ankle annoyed me as she brushed the arch of her now-free foot against it. I examined her hair, a confined firework of an

Afro, and her shoulders under the crimson tank top that completed her ensemble. I tried not to stare at her. I knew it would be lovely. And arrogant.

Instead, too preoccupied now to attend the talk, I scrawled a drawing into my notebook; only a few rapid, furious lines: pointed cat-face, long back, tail. Slash-slash-slash for stripes. Tiger. Then there's the squat, rounded, low-to-the-ground, long-lined nose. Badger.

The segment concluded and I grabbed my stuff in quick disorganization, out the door before I'd even put my bag on properly.

She caught up with me on the college green. She'd taken off her heels and was holding them in one hand by the straps. Her feet stood out against the grass as if they belonged there.

"Hey," she said. "Are you running late for something?" “No—”

"I was only in a rush," she said on my behalf. I could detect a grin in her voice and swiftly looked up to capture its edge. Her face was stunning. And arrogant. She was certain of herself and what she believed she understood.

"I have a lot of work to do."

"I could make out some of what you were sketching. n of of of of of of of of

I didn't respond. I accelerated my pace. My notebook fought its way out of my arms and she grabbed it before it struck the ground. I came to a halt, hesitant to ask for it back, and started placing the items I'd been carrying into my bag. Then I stood there, without reaching for my notepad.

She opened the cover after looking at me. The photographs were along, across, and over my notes. Animals, animals, and more animals. Small, large, predators, and prey. Women's bodies in and out hinted at and begun. Most were shattered in some fashion, with limbs twisting and elongating, heads disappearing, and legs twisted at weird angles. A few were visibly changing, their feet sprouting claws and fur sprouting.

The term "electronic commerce" refers to the sale of electronic goods.

"You're fantastic," she remarked. "How do you get such good grades in Anthro if this is all you do in class?"

"I don't do well in school," I admitted.

"You do," she urged gently. "I saw your exam paper when it was returned to me last week."

I placed the notepad inside my bag, zipped it up, and began walking again. She remained where she was.

"Hey, I moved into Forest House this semester," she yelled after me. If you wanted, I'm sure we'd offer you some commissions. They've been talking about putting up murals and paintings, and this would be ideal."

Forest House was a co-op made up largely of lesbian witches. Bitches. They were girls playing with toys and calling it real life. My gorge rose just thinking about those babes and their crystals and their spirit animal totem stuff. I gulped it once more.

"This weekend, we're throwing a party. If you wish to stop by."
I turned back to look at her. She was still there, stunning, haughty, and optimistic. Her scarlet shoes hung from her fingertips. She was not petite. She took up space and she grinned.
"Fuck Forest House," I yelled out loudly enough for her to hear. I turned around again and hurried back to my dorm room.
My dorm did not have a co-op. It was concrete and towering, uninteresting to the sight and the touch, yet insulating, which is what I wanted of it. I hurried up the stairs to my room and flung my bag on the floor. The room was tiny and cramped, but I enjoyed it. It was decked, colorful scarves spilled and hanging everywhere. I had acquired some of those washable wall crayons and wrote lines and colors all over the wall, but no apparent forms like in my notebook. It's no use gazing at particular proposals all the time. I felt comfortable in the room, yet no one except myself ever came in.

I fell onto the floor, onto a braided rug created by one of my aunts, round and swirling and a touch scratchy. I removed my jacket, shirt, and bra and laid on the mat with my stomach and breasts crushed against it. My nipples were scraped by the prickly soft granules. I pushed open my pants and slid my hand inside. My vulva and clit felt heated and swollen. The term "electronic commerce" refers to the sale of electronic goods. I massaged till my breath came rapid, pressing my breasts harder into the carpeting. I slid over onto my back and arched into the carpeting. My first two fingers stroked hard and slowly down and up, then focussed, circling and circling my clit through the cloth.

My breathing ceased. I strained against my palm, gulped in more air, and rushed forward in quick, quivering surges.

"Fuck, fuck, fuck," I murmured. I stood up, and wiped my forehead with one hand, leaving my pants on the floor with my shirt and bra. It hadn't been enough: not the type of excitement that would be satiated with orgasms, nor the kind of wrath that I could quell with weird outbursts on the green. My body was shaking under the skin, much beneath. The fundamental level, which nearly no one can see. Muscles and bones tremble.

There is an entire code within your body, everything working together to keep you who you are. Every cell cooperates, participates, lives, and dies according to this so that you remain perceptibly yourself. Isn't everyone aware of this?

My code is messed up. My code is enchanted. I don't stay myself.

There is no central point.

My whole body trembled and convulsed. I was lying on the bed. The agony began, like a wild burn-itch all through me, like a muscle you want to stretch, a cramp you can't get rid of, pain building and unrelenting. I was absorbed and I panted in it.

Then compression. Tiny, small, small. Twitching, quivering. Settling. Now comes the relief. No more suffering. There are no more words. Hunger. A racing heart. Fast. The answer is yes. Skitter. Forever. Food. A little gap. Squeeze. Fast. Run, run, run. Fear, frozen. Tremendous eyes, big heat, close to me. Dread, fear, fear. Claws at me, soaring. The answer is yes. Fast fast. Run.

I found myself nude and drenched in perspiration and minor scratches in the basement of my hostel. I rushed swiftly, maybe too fast, and discovered the basic pullover dress I'd stashed beneath the washing machine. I attempted to keep my garments widely distributed and accessible, but of course, it was hit or miss. I scented my flesh and tried to remember as much as I could. I looked around and discovered a little mound of droppings with a finger. I despised mouse-times. Mouse times were perilous and terrifying, particularly because some jerks persisted in bringing kittens into their dorm rooms. But, in reality, all times were perilous and frightening to me and others. Even woman-times. Maybe woman-times the most, since that's when I knew.

On wobbly legs, I made my way back up to my hall. I sneaked into the bathroom and bathed, then put my dress back over my wet body and hurried back to my own room. Despite the oppressive heat, I climbed into bed and slept.

The following day, I discovered a Forest House party flier among hundreds of other flyers on a corkboard. It was light pink and had a design of a lady who seemed to be transforming into a tree, her curves twisting and sensuous, fusing with bark and trunk and pressing into the earth. The poster on the side of the tree lady stated, in huge letters, FUN FUN FUN. FALL MIXER AT THE FOREST HOUSE, SATURDAY DECEMBER 18TH, 10-??? The poster made me grin, then chuckle. I caressed the tree lady with a finger and drew her outside lines. What would it be like to be a tree person, a plant person? Is it safer to hurry to the earth and establish roots, hoping to grow big enough not to be stomped on or eaten? Perhaps it was all more or less the same. Still, I loved her impulsively; she seemed to have freedom and joy that I did not. I removed the poster and hid it in my room.

For minutes together, later that week, looking at the tree woman's form in half darkness, touching my own body and rising and falling, sea-like, I felt something like forgiveness for those crystal-wielding, herb-taking, cunt-licking bitches who prayed, secretly and openly, for the changing of their limbs and the release of animal-selves, animal-muscles.

Even as I opened, climbed, came, and came again, I turned off the sense of forgiveness as it neared me.

I went to the party. The term "electronic commerce" refers to the sale of electronic goods. The garment was a bit of a prank. Women and a few enigmatic men lingered in doorways, sipping spiced ales and fruit wines and softly caressing. There were candles, incense, and a few rings of individuals actively performing charms. I saw a lady on all fours near a sofa, arching her back and making a growling noise. I took a few steps closer to her. She was completely white, with reddish-brown hair. Polly, but a touch skinnier. She gazed at me, human eyes all dilated, and hissed. I took another step back.

"She's completely obsessed with her wolf totem." I turned around and saw one of the lads, his face a tangle of acne but friendly beneath. "It's a little strange at first, isn't it? But don't worry, if she becomes too wild, we can touch her with silver and she'll come back." He extended his arm to show me the tiny silver band around his wrist. I reached out my hand and touched it, sliding my finger over the surface. I lifted my gaze to his, drew back the curtain slightly, and grinned.

He quickly departed the discussion after that. The wolf girl had become sleepy and was curled up on the floor at the end of the sofa, wriggling her butt as if she had a tail. I walked through the home, down the hall to the stairway, turning away.

"Hello," she said, startling me. She down the steps from the first level, mainly in shadow. I observed her outline: hair, shoulders, hips. On the first floor, she emerged into the light. She was dressed in a navy-blue dress that was basic but as tight and sensual as everything else she wore. She wore it casually, wore the bulge of her ass and her breasts like they were simple to bear, nothing to fret about. But she was still wearing heels, this time in brown faux snakeskin. Her feet seemed to be shading up from them, the lighter bottom visible against the tan, ascending to the darker brown of her top skin. Her feet were so much safer to gaze at, but not that safe. It was also strange to constantly look at someone's feet.

"I'm delighted you showed up," she replied. I stared at her face, her eyes.
Her expression was not haughty. They were inviting, open, and dark.
"I saw someone dressed as a wolf," I added, without knowing why.
Her grin sprang out like the sun breaking through a storm. "Some folks are a bit flashy about their magic.
You want a beer or something?"
"All OK," I responded. The term "independent" refers to a person who does not work for the government. I saw her broad back and the swing of her ass. She came back with two drinks. I drank and swallowed the bitterness.
"Look, I know you're a senior, right?" she said. So you came before me, and I'm guessing you used to hang out at Forest House, and—"
"Not really," I said.
"But you maybe knew Polly." She was nervous now, peering down into her beer can. "I heard she was kinda—she could be a

horrible bitch, particularly to the ladies she slept around with. So I assumed that's why you dislike Forest House. I'm delighted you came, and I'm sorry if anything screwed up happened to you here."

My skin began to vibrate. Twice in a week, Jesus? That was unusual. I laid my drink down, gently, against the wall. That made it less likely that someone would kick it over.

"I have to go," I said. "I'm sorry, I'm sorry."

"No, it's not—I just have to leave." I started to make my way through the mob. Right now I felt buzzing, tingling, a type of pre-painful discomfort in muscles and joints. It will soon be more, but I knew I had time to get away. As I approached the door, a sharp cramp struck, and I came to a halt, my hand on the doorpost, bending, waiting.

"How are you?" It was the previous silver-bracelet man. "You should get some water and sit down for a bit."

"Not drunk," I said. I shoved his solicitous hand away and walked out the door. I was sweating despite the cold night. The pain in my feet, knees, ass, and back became more intense. I ran with a peculiar, loping pace, encouraged by hurry but hampered by pain and bone strain. There was an almost-forest at the border of campus—deep enough to hide for a time, not deep enough for much hunting, assuming it was a hunter approaching. I could make it.

I raced panting, perspiration streaming down my neck and back. The term "electronic commerce" refers to the sale of electronic goods. I unzipped my hoodie and let it fall. I reached down and took off my shoes; my feet were all pins and needles and longed to be free. n of of of of of of of of of. For a minute I imagined I knew a wolf-time was approaching and I chuckled to be so suggestible. My tongue became heavy in my mouth, my thoughts skewed, and I knelt over, almost on all fours but not quite touching the earth in front of me. I was going quicker now, faster than a lady could. I was at the trees and suddenly the agony was blinding for a minute and then I was sleek, sleek, swift, energy straight through, shooting silver out to ground and pleasure— Joy of movement, the pleasure of speed, pleasure of sweat on fur, heavy pleasure, feet rapid and fragrance all around. Nothing to worry about, everything is moving, sniffing, listening, and pausing. Yes, hunger in the mouth, stomach, and pit. Turning and turning, smelling silence and eagerness. Yes, other-kill growl gobble spin chase. The smell of not-prey, smell, too-strong, melt disappears. Marking, sniffing, moving. Still not-prey. Smelling. Knowing.

I know. I'm still here. Looking. Stillness. In her silence, I looked at her. Surface, you're alive. Fear and pleasure. The answer is yes. At her side, she spreads her fingers. I'd want to smell them. Step by step. We're almost there. Raise your nose. Nose to fingertips. The fragrance is strong and deep. Sweat and the brass taste of her menstrual cycle. I can see her with fresh clarity. It must be coyote season. Woman- time things flow through in coyote-time. I preserve my calm and her eyes. Then I run.

When I regained consciousness, I was huddled at the far edge of the woodland. I sat, tired, in my own sweat, moss and dry leaves brushing up on my knees and thighs. I sat there for a time, letting my breathing settle down, muscles trembling beneath my skin. Then I realized. Was she really there? Had I made it up? I turned around, slowly, rising to my feet. In the early morning light, I could hardly see. The hardest aspect of womanhood was that I couldn't smell anything. Humans can't smell for shit.

I believed my clothing was closer to campus, maybe damaged but still usable. I began going back carefully, stroking the trees as I went. After a lengthy change, a full night like that one, I was always both fatigued and oddly refreshed.

The rising sun was warm and brilliant. I stood there watching it fill in all the night grays of the almost forest.

Back to my clothing, she was asleep against a tree, the tatters of my Harry Potter shirt tucked under her arm. I attempted to wear largely clothing I didn't care about, although I felt perverted at times. I stood there watching her, the pull of her party dress over her boobs and tummy, the fabric carelessly sliding up her thighs. In the crook of her elbow, I examined my shirt. She blinked her eyes open. We were each watching each other.

I grabbed her shirt, analyzing the tension, the tear produced by a claw as I pushed my way free. I pulled it over my head. I began to walk away.

"Your jeans are over there," she pointed out.

I saw them and proceeded towards them. "Wait," she advised. in case...

I locked my gaze on her. "You're not afraid," I charged. "You should be."

"I'm terrified," she said.

"You like it, it makes you on." "Yeah," she agreed.

"It's fucking terrifying crap," I said. "This isn't a game. I transform into many animals; did you assume I was a werewolf like that foolish girl? She is nothing; she is just a human being who enjoys being psychedelic and odd."

"Do I look like a coyote right now?" “No.” She laughed.

I exhaled a sigh. I drew myself into a squat. I was exhausted. "I'm dozens of various sorts of animals," I replied. "Some of them, I'm not even sure are genuine. Some are unquestionably extinct. When I change, I don't always know who I am, what my English name is, or what others think about me. I can't make it stop, typically, and I don't determine when it occurs, and there's no rule, that I can tell, except that—it happens when I'm feeling something. Not one thing in particular, just—strong stuff. And even then, not always. "I'm not sure why." She gave a nod. I took a deep breath, sank my fingers into my hands, and spoke quickly. "When Polly broke up with me, I transformed into a beast. I also scratched her. Badly. That is why she transferred."

She burst out laughing. I gave her a sidelong glance. Then I burst out laughing. I chuckled as I landed fully on the earth with a jolt.

"It was horrible," I said after I'd finished laughing. "I mean, she was a b*tch, she truly was, but I assaulted her. As a teddy bear. It's not..."

"You didn't murder her," she clarified. "I mean, you may have, but you didn't."

"Bully for me," I said. "I really mean it."

"You don't seem to be terrified."

"I am," she said. She leaned out and touched my thigh. She crept up and stroked her fingers through my pubic hair, this way and that, her gaze lifting to mine. "I'm terrified," she said. She clasped her fingers over my vulva, and I could feel it warm and expand under them. "Is this okay?" She waited a minute. "It turns me on because it's amazing and because it's yours."

I kept my voice low. The throb and pulse pushed out from my chest to her hand. She snatched her hand away.

"I want to fuck you," I murmured, gazing at the grass beneath my fingers and not at her. "When I see you in class, the insightful things you say, you get beneath the skin of things. And your hair, and your feet in those high heels, and your clothing. The contours of your ass and your boobs and your belly. Your jaw form, as well as the strength of your back. This creature I am shouldn't fuck anybody. But I really want to fuck you."

As I talked, I could hear her breathing, and suddenly she was all over me, jumping and pushing and tumbling me back onto the floor of the almost forest. Her fingers returned to my labia and my clit, dragging me up into her like a magnet. My back arched and my hips thrust forward. She bit and scratched me with her other hand, and I laughed hopelessly before becoming silent.

I sensed silence, swirling, and a big, violent hunger in the core of my body, drawing away my breath and returning it in spurts. The sounds in my throat were weird yet human, for all their severity. Her middle finger dipped and played with the entrance of my cunt, teasing the puckered edge and sending a thrill straight to her palm on my clit. My hips surged and bobbed like a toy boat in a raging tide, and I came in sharp, pulsating jolts before forcing myself back, down, away.

"Take off your dress," I urged hoarsely, and she did as she gazed at me. Her underwear was a basic cotton bikini and her bra was purple and satiny. She removed her bra and took her under- wear off. I was on her breasts as soon as I could see them, a raisin-colored nipple squeezed hard between my lips. She produced a rapid, deep, grunting sound, and then a higher, floating wail. She regained her breath. "Your period's going to start," I informed her. "I could detect it."

She smiled softly and breathlessly, but for the first time, I saw a pang of dread in her eyes. She didn't try to disguise it; she simply stared at me while pressing her back against a tree trunk and parting her thighs.

"I want it deep and leisurely," she said.

I took in the form and soft folds that encircled me as I circled her breasts with my tongue and her cunt with my fingers.

Larger and more rounded than mine. I brushed my fingers over the top of her clit, felt her tremble, and pushed in harder, circling and finding the smooth and warm entrance. I straddled her thigh and pushed my cunt against her, releasing flashes of color beneath my skin all over. My thoughts twisted and split, and I let my first two fingers slip into her, deep and slow. Her arm wrapped over my back and hugged me tightly. I squeezed her deeply, inside and out, the heel of my palm and my thumb seeking for her clit. I fell to the side of her after losing my balance against her leg. I closed my eyes and then opened them again to see her face. Her lips were widening, and she was almost silently pushing against my fingers. She laughed, unexpectedly, and then choked on the end of it, and I felt her tighten and rise and come, the tension in her exploding like a bubble, opening like the new leaf on a tree, fresh, green, strongly attached.

I yanked my fingers out of her, showed her the blood on the tips, and then sucked them clean with my lips. I couldn't have said anything more threatening, warning, daring or accepting. Woman-time is devoid of words. Her gaze was fixed on mine, and as I ate her blood, her eyes lighted up as if I had touched her. She gasped and pulled me back, clutching my ass, pushing my hips toward her, and forcing her face into my crotch, nuzzling and licking before rising to kiss my lips. She remained there, long and delicious and dizzying, and her hand moved between my knees and stroked me till I came back, effortlessly, without struggle, fire-bursts in a display I didn't have to manage.

We lay on the ground thereafter, apart and silent, our fingertips touching. Finally, I rose up and started hunting for my jeans. We got dressed, still quiet. She brushed a few leaves from her hair, leaned against a tree trunk, and stared at me again. Her eyes were asking questions. I wanted to respond to them. Something with wings was lingering in the distance, not quite here.

"Will you come back with me?" I said. "I want to show you my room."

She clutched my palm till I could feel the bones underneath.

"Yes," she said. “Yes.”

Chapter 5

There would have been a celebration if her father had his way. Victoria had declined his offer of something lavish and grand to welcome her home after six years in the South.

She was aware that he meant well and that she was too elderly to go to parties. Since her Sweet Sixteen and since she was twelve, Victoria hadn't indulged in one. She was now an adult—she was 24 years old. She had the legal right to vote, smoke, and consume alcohol. Additionally, she had completed all of those tasks. She had five boyfriends and even shattered a few hearts.

However, she wasn't really able to inform her father about it.

She was unable to speak to her father at this time since he was sitting across from her and feeding them hearty portions of a salmon casserole.

He continued, leaning back in his chair and folding his arms, "Tell me if you like it."

Victoria nodded as she picked up a little portion of food from her plate to chew.

"Good job, Daddy. Did you succeed?
Like his ceramics and the woodworking dad had dabbled in after her mother passed away, she reasoned that it may have been something he picked up while she was abroad. After all, in her free time, Victoria had experimented with body painting and taken images of beautiful ladies in their underwear.
However, her father said, "I didn't make it. Pam acted. a fresh girlfriend? No. He would have spoken out.
Victoria raised an eyebrow in hazy recognition. Oh, right.
She referred to that caterer.
Dad gave a nod. "Right. I request that she bring meals for our meetings.
Well, she did a terrific job, Victoria said after taking another piece of the dish.
Her father was as thrilled about it as if he had created it himself. "She's consented to

offer you a few suggestions in the kitchen," he said.
Victoria gulped down her first mouthful. “Agreed?”
"Yes, I guess. She suggested—"I ran into her in town one day and I noted that you would be returning home soon and you weren't very acquainted with a kitchen's procedures."
"She proposed?"
Okay, I enquired. What damage, therefore, is there? Making potato salad and frying some chicken sometimes wouldn't do any harm.
Victoria let go of her fork and relaxed her shoulders. "So this is about your continuous adoration of deep-fried chicken?"
Half-laughing, her father. How should I begin? I like eating fried chicken.
Everyone had their shortcomings, Victoria reasoned, therefore it was acceptable. Hers was a tall, golden lady with lovely, muscular legs.

She saw her father speaking once again.

"Surely none of those Georgian females you made friends with roasted a chicken in front of you or prepared a bowl of macaroni?"

Victoria curled her lips in contemplation. Yes, she had encountered several Southern females and had learned many delightful things from them, but none of them included a stove or a pot.

However, her father wouldn't want to hear that. Neither Mindy, Sylvia, nor even Bethany gave a damn about the fact that she couldn't cook.

Victoria decided to leave it alone since it would be absurd in his eyes and something she learned in school.

In addition, he was so chuffed with himself that it was almost endearing, and Victoria could tell he wanted the same excitement from her by the hopefulness in his eyes and the twitch in the corner of his mouth.

Victoria took another piece of the creamy stew while grinning broadly.

Just let me know when, Daddy, she murmured, shaking her head.

Victoria chose a tank top and jeans since she wasn't precisely sure what to wear to a culinary class. Pam arrived at the door wearing shorts and a T-shirt. Pam lived in a modest cottage outside of town.

Due to the way Pam's long legs protruded from under her shorts, Victoria believed they were the perfect fit for Pam. In fact, Victoria reasoned as she examined Pam's brown knees, she may suggest to her that she think about never again donning a pair of pants.

Pam's hair had a rebellious kink that protruded from her head in fuzzy curls that she had colored strawberry blonde, but Victoria had never noticed this. Pam also had plump, rosy, and moist lips without any lip gloss. She had two silver hoops in each ear and a little diamond earring in her left nostril.

Pam had a lilac scent. Victoria thought it may be powder. She may have inquired, but she didn't really know Pam; all she knew was that she was a few years older and kept to herself.

Therefore, Victoria extended her hand and introduced herself rather than stating all of the above.

"My name is Victoria," she introduced herself. "My father says you could teach me a thing or two."

Pam grinned. "I'm not sure whether that's true, but I promised him I'd show you some of what I know."

Victoria was permitted in.

Pam's vivid furniture choices, the orange wing-backed chairs, and the golden sofa drew Victoria's attention. Her coffee table and curio were made of dark wood. Her hardwood floors were spotless and gleaming.

Victoria stayed behind Pam, her ears perked up to music gently playing in the background, something jazzy by a lady with a deep, raspy voice. They arrived in Pam's spacious kitchen, where she had a variety of bowls and pans on display.

"I don't generally offer lessons, but your papa was insistent, going on about woman's responsibilities and such. "Are you getting married or something?" Pam arched her brow.

Victoria shook her head and chuckled.

Pam went on. "Well, at any rate, I felt I could keep things simple and show you meat and potatoes, fried chicken and gravy, but that would be an obvious waste of time and energy. I'd rather show you those really exquisite recipes for those special occasions, for romantic evenings when you want to wow someone special. Such like this."

Pam handed Victoria a tiny dish filled with dark, oval-shaped fruit and lightly shaved nuts. Her nose was filled with the lovely aroma of coconut rum.

"Those are figs," Pam said. "I put them in the fridge overnight to soak. "Please take one."

Victoria took a bite out of the fig. The fruit and rum liquids danced on her tongue, tickled her throat, and warmed her chest. The crunchy almonds provide a lovely contrast to the richness of the figs and rum.

"I'm going to make a fig rum bread with them."

Victoria spent approximately an hour and a half in Pam's kitchen for this short course. Victoria laughed as she walked away because she was hungry.

Pam had informed Victoria that the loaf needed to rest for twenty-four hours before it could be eaten, so she strolled home, deciding she'd have a turkey sandwich later.

Perhaps it was the rum. Perhaps it was the jazz. But late that night, as Victoria lay alone in her bed, she recalled the taste of rum and the fragrance of coconut, she remembered gorgeous brown legs and a head of curly, golden hair, and she spread her legs and reached down, thinking about Pam, and she pleasured herself until she felt exhausted.

Pam was an excellent instructor. After all, she'd lived on this planet for thirty-one years. Victoria had seen and done so much that her brief stay in Georgia seemed little in contrast.

Pam waved the fresh herbs in front of Victoria's nose, and she sniffed them. Pam had determined that because Victoria was still burning rice after two weeks of instruction, they should meet three times a week rather than two.

It didn't worry Victoria. She'd become used to sitting at Pam's table, standing in front of her stove, and leaning on her counter.

Pam was now setting aside the herbs and squeezing lime over a pan of prawns.

"You have to be cautious when cooking with citrus," Pam said. "It has a tendency to dry out your meals. But the shrimp will cook quickly anyhow, so we don't have to worry about it."

Victoria, on the other hand, was more interested in rubbing the lime on Pam's lips and sucking the leftovers off.

"You know, Victoria, if you don't start paying attention, you won't be much better a chef than the day you stepped into this kitchen," Pam stated as she realized she was still admiring Pam's lips.

Victoria shook her head. She grabbed Pam's waist and continued to disregard the remark. "Has anybody ever told you that for someone who cooks so well, you're extremely thin?"

Pam drew her chin in. "Perhaps it's because I nibble." "And you're never still."

And Victoria never stopped looking at her. Pam walked from the stove to the island in the center of her kitchen, then from the table to the sink. Victoria saw Pam's sweat running down her neck, her calves flexing and releasing, and the muscles in her lean arms contracting as she carried pots and casseroles.

"And how about you? "How do you stay in such excellent shape?"

Victoria sucked her bottom lip. "My father appears to believe I'm growing by the minute."
"And what are your thoughts?"
"I guess I like to eat, and whatever I put in my mouth sits like a pair of saddlebags on my hips."
Victoria couldn't be sure, but she suspected Pam looked down at her hips for confirmation.
And it was at that point that Victoria chose to kiss Pam.
It was only a simple neck kiss. Victoria was positive it wouldn't harm her. And maybe Pam won't even notice. And even if she didn't notice, she probably wouldn't mind a tongue on her silky collarbone or a hand on her elbow that moved down her arm and closed loosely around her wrist.
Pam, as it turned out, didn't mind any of this. Pam sighed as if this was exactly what she had been hoping for all along. So Victoria grabbed her waist and pulled her

close. She gave her a kiss on the lips. They shared the lime flavor on their tongues.

Victoria knelt in front of Pam, her face brushing against the front of her flowery dress. Victoria raised the garment and gathered it around Pam's waist. Pam's stomach was kissed on either side, and she sucked softly on her navel.

They eventually made their way down to Pam's kitchen floor.

Pam's dress was carefully removed and pushed over her head, revealing her red panties.

Victoria's eyes welled up with tears at the notion of her seducing Pam. Pam, on the other hand, was beaming.

Pam arched her back as she felt Victoria's tongue on her nipples. The soft feeling of Victoria's breath on her lobe made her laugh. Pam appeared on her own kitchen floor when Victoria scented the hint of lime and could no longer smell the shrimp, a sure indicator that the supper was over.

Pam was kissed on the knees as Victoria brushed her fingers around the softest portions of her thighs.
"I'm hungry," she said quietly.

"So, you learning much over there?" said Victoria's father as she sat in her father's kitchen, thinking about Pam.
"Yes, I'm learning a lot," Victoria responded with a grin.
In reality, she had only lately discovered that Pam was rather ticklish, that the tile on her kitchen floor was six different colors, that Pam's favorite color was blue, that her cottage was passed down from her great-grandmother, and, most importantly, that Pam liked strawberries.
Last night, Victoria fed them to her after they had tumbled about nude in Pam's bed for over two hours. They had eaten strawberries and sipped champagne all

night, and Victoria had remained the whole time.

Her father nodded, pleased. "All OK," he said. "You'll have to make something for me shortly."

"Yes, Daddy," Victoria confirmed. "I'll make you something shortly."

He then gently squeezed her arm.

"It seems like you are doing a bit more eating than cooking, in my view."

Victoria struggled to restrain herself from flushing. Pam had said that she appreciated her additional fluffiness. It made her feel warm and juicy.

And Victoria felt heated as she considered seeing Pam in three hours. The sensation between her legs was juicy as she imagined Pam coming to the door and welcoming her nude.

Victoria stretched and leaned back in her chair.

It was meant to be almond-crusted tilapia, but Victoria had overcooked the tiny pieces of fish, causing them to stick to the bottom of the pan due to a lack of olive oil, thus the only thing salvageable was the almonds.

Pam placed them on her lips and slid them inside her mouth with her tongue, while Victoria watched.

"I also burnt Daddy's ribs," Victoria said. Pam burst out laughing. "I'm sure he wasn't bothered."

Victoria made a shaky motion with her head. "No, he was irritated. He likes BBQ. He informed me three times that I had "ruined a pretty nice hunk of pork."

Pam laughed. "You'll make amends to him. I'll make you a tray that you can pass off as your own."

Victoria shook her head. “Maybe. But I'm not sure whether it'll fly. I'll need to start explaining myself shortly. All these classes and all I'm actually learning is how to set off smoke alarms."

Pam got closer. "Surely you've learned more than that, Victoria."

And she took Victoria's hand in hers and put it between her thighs. Pam raised it so that Victoria's hand rested on her cunt.
Victoria felt comfortable there. Victoria, too, was welcoming. Victoria was soon no longer concerned about the fish. She soon found herself in Pam's bed, kissing her fingers, shoulders, and knees.
Pam tasted better than anything Victoria could have imagined putting in her tongue. Pam was both bitter and delicious, delicate and wet.
And as Pam brushed up against Victoria's lips, Victoria felt stuffed, as if she'd eaten five times in the core of Pam's hips.

They often spoke afterward, which is how Victoria discovered Pam was a Gemini who grew up in Syracuse and was never properly taught to cook. It was also how Victoria found out Pam was departing for Paris in six weeks.

Pam's heavy brows had been smoothed out by Victoria. But suddenly she swiftly lowered her hand, as if she had been burned.

Pam would be individually taught by French Chef Something-or-Other, and while Pam went on and on about it, Victoria gazed at her, looking for any indication of regret that she had to speak the words, or even better, that she suddenly changed her mind and decided to remain after all.

Pam, on the other hand, simply continued chatting.

"An opening appeared out of nowhere. And I've been telling myself that it's too late, that I'm too old for any more lessons, that I already know all I need to know, yet it's a highly sought-after profession. I'd be an idiot to decline."

The joy in Pam's voice made Victoria grin despite herself.

"I understand, honey," she responded. If I were you, I would absolutely go for it."

Victoria simply spoke the words because she felt compelled to. She spoke the words because she was about to weep. Victoria was twenty-four years old, which was just too old to weep.

Pam was speaking once again. Her voice had become faint and harsh.

"How do you think your papa would feel about it?" she asked Victoria.

Victoria hoped Pam wouldn't notice the difference in her voice. She prayed the tears wouldn't slide down her cheeks and onto Pam's arm.

"Well, I know he likes your fried chicken, but he'll find another caterer for his meetings," Victoria said.

Pam burst out laughing. "You stupid girl. I'm referring to you. I'm referring to you leaving with me. "How would he react to that?"

Victoria buried her head into Pam's crook and savored the delicate lilac aroma from her skin.

No, Victoria wasn't sure how her father would react, but she imagined herself waking up in a different location with Pam, eating new and interesting things that Pam would make for her, and feeding her with her hands. Already, Victoria saw herself whispering things in broken French into Pam's ear.

Victoria agreed that maybe, yes, every young lady should learn to cook as she cut red potatoes, put in fresh onions, and added sour cream and mayonnaise. She'd finally figured it out.

She shook her green bean pot. She wrapped the pound cake she had left to chill.

Her father would be pleased with the lunch, and he would be quite proud of her. He'd also like fried chicken.

He'd be pleased with the entire affair.

Also, Paris. He'd get over it, and maybe one day he'd even be happy. Victoria arranged the table well, with a six-pack of her father's favorite beer in a bucket of ice.

Victoria hoped she could see the expression on his face.

Instead, she'd be sitting in Pam's convertible's passenger seat. And she and Pam would be on the aircraft by the time he found the message.

Victoria and her boyfriend would arrive in Paris seven hours later. Pam would acquire French culinary techniques, and Victoria would find new ways to love Pam.

And Victoria understood that this was the most essential lesson of all.

www.ingramcontent.com/pod-product-compliance
Lightning Source LLC
LaVergne TN
LVHW052045160826
845678LV00015B/3119
9798370658419